Snow White and the Seven Aliens

ORCHARD BOOKS
96 Leonard Street, London EC2A 4RH
Orchard Books Australia
14 Mars Road, Lane Cove, NSW 2066
First published in Great Britain in 1998
First paperback publication 1999
Text © Laurence Anholt 1998
Illustrations © Arthur Robins 1998
The rights of Laurence Anholt to be identified as the author
and Arthur Robins as the illustrator of this work have been
asserted by them in accordance with the Copyright, Designs
and Patents Act, 1988.
A CIP catalogue record for this book is available
from the British Library.
1 86039 610 0 (hardback)
1 86039 650 X (paperback)
Printed in Great Britain

Snow White and the Seven Aliens

Written by Laurence Anholt
Illustrated by Arthur Robins

These stories have not been tested on animals.

 ORCHARD BOOKS

Snow White dreamed of becoming a
pop-star. She wanted to be number one in
the charts, just like her hero, Hank Hunk
from Boysnog.

Snow White had a beautiful voice. She
was a great dancer too. And she could even
write her own songs.

Only one thing stood in her way – her
wicked stepmother.

Once upon a time Snow White's stepmother had been a famous pop-star. She had been the Mean Queen, lead singer in The Wonderful Wicked Witches. But now her voice was croaky and she was no longer a star. She had become mad with jealousy of Snow White.

"You will never be famous like me!" she would hiss. "You look too…ordinary. You don't even have a band. And besides, your nose is too small."

Then, the Mean Queen would storm
out of the room, leaving poor Snow White
to weep under the Boysnog posters in
her bedroom.

Snow White's father was a kind little
man. He liked doing jigsaw puzzles and
making small Plasticine models. Although
he loved his daughter, he was not strong
enough to stand up to his wife.

The Mean Queen had a huge dressing-room at the top of the house, with dozens of mirrors and shelves of make-up, as if she were still a great star.

And sometimes she forced her poor husband to sit behind the dressing-table mirror and tell her that she was still beautiful.

Mirror, mirror, on the wall,
Who has the cutest nose of all?

From behind the mirror, her terrified husband would reply:

Then, the Mean Queen would scream with laughter and march around the house croaking her ancient songs, and remembering the day when The Wonderful Wicked Witches had appeared on the Christmas edition of Top of the Pops.

Now, Snow White often sat in the garden surrounded by little birdies and bunny rabbits, singing quietly in her beautiful clear voice. When she looked down, the Mean Queen would almost choke with rage.

Day by day, the Mean Queen could see
that Snow White was growing into a very
beautiful young woman. With that tiny
pink nose…how the Mean Queen hated her.

Only the mirror brought her comfort.

And the mirror would reply:

And so it went on. Until, one terrible night, Snow White's father could stand the lies no longer. The Mean Queen demanded:

Mirror, mirror above the sink,

Tell me what you REALLY think.

It's time you started coming clean—
CHOOSE SNOW WHITE—
OR ME, YOUR QUEEN.

In a tiny, trembling voice, the mirror replied:

All right. I've really had enough,
I'm fed up with the lies and stuff.
You are past it, old and sad,
Crinkly, wrinkly - really bad.
Your nose is sort of long and hairy,
Beside you, Snow White
is a Christmas fairy!

The Mean Queen leapt to her feet. With a sweep of her bony hand, she sent her make-up and bottles of perfume crashing to the floor. She seized her husband by his collar, and lifted him off his feet.

"Get Snow White OUT OF MY HOUSE," she spat into his terrified face. "Make sure she NEVER EVER returns."

The poor man crawled towards the door.
But the Mean Queen had one more order –
something so terrible that her husband
quaked in his sandals.

To prove that Snow White has really gone... BRING ME THAT TINY SNUBBY NOSE ON A COCKTAIL STICK!!!
AH, HA, HA, HAH HA HA-A-A-RRR!!!

And so, Snow White's father led his beautiful daughter far into the wild and dangerous city. With tears streaming down his face, he bought her an all-day bus pass and kissed his sweet daughter goodbye.

Of course, he could not bring himself to cut off that precious snubby nose, so he quickly modelled a false one out of some pink Plasticine which he always carried in his pocket.

This he brought back to the Mean Queen
on a cocktail stick.

When the Mean Queen saw the little
nose, she screamed with laughter all over
again. Then she did something so ghastly
that her husband felt quite ill.

She took the Plasticine nose, dipped it in mayonnaise and ATE IT, served with a side salad and French fries.

"Mmm!!" she said, licking her lips. "Tasty!"

Meanwhile, poor Snow White wandered through the city, lost and alone.

It grew dark, and she started to feel afraid. Then, in the distance, she saw a dim green light between the buildings. Faint with hunger, she stumbled towards it and found herself in a clearing by a car park.

There in front of her was…a gleaming silver spacecraft!

A little ladder led up to a door where a flashing neon sign said:

SWINGING SPACESHIP
NIGHT CLUB.

Under this was pinned another smaller notice. This one read:

Cleaner wanted. Apply within.

Too tired to feel afraid, Snow White pushed the bell. Quietly, the door slid open and she stepped nervously inside.

And so it was that Snow White began her new life as a cleaner at the Swinging Spaceship Night Club. The hours were long, the pay was poor, but at least some good bands played from time to time.

"Who knows?" sighed Snow White. "Perhaps I might even hear Hank Hunk from Boysnog one day!"

One evening, Snow White was told to prepare the dressing-room for a special band who would be playing that night.

In the dressing-room she found seven identical chairs. Laid neatly on the seven identical chairs were seven identical space helmets.

I wonder who will be changing in here? she thought.

Just then, she heard strange voices singing outside in the corridor…

"Hi ho, hi ho, it's off to space we go…"

What an awful song, thought Snow White. I wonder who wrote those terrible lyrics?

The door opened and in stepped seven of the most extraordinary creatures Snow White had ever seen.

"Hi," said the first stranger. "We are the Seven Aliens. We are booked to perform tonight. We are number 4,324 in the pop charts, you know. Meet the band..."

"And what about you?" laughed Snow White, pointing at the very funny-looking alien who had spoken to her first. "What is your name?"

"He's BOTTY!!" shouted all the other aliens together.

"Well," giggled Snow White. "I am very pleased to meet you. Now, if you like, I will polish your space helmets before you go on stage."

While Snow White polished, she sang a sad and beautiful song. The Seven Aliens were entranced.

"That was wonderful," gurgled Grotty when she had finished. "Tell us your name."
"I am Snow White," said Snow White.

"Oh, Snow White," sniffed Snotty. "The truth is, we cannot sing for toffee and the only words we can think of are 'hi ho, hi ho'. If you would join our band, we would blast up the charts like a rocket into space."

And so it was that
Snow White and the
Seven Aliens played
their very first gig
at the Swinging
Spaceship
Night Club.

Meanwhile, at home, Snow White's father wept over his lost daughter until his jigsaw puzzles were soggy. The Mean Queen, on the other hand, was in a very good mood. She went to admire herself in her magic mirror.

Mirror, mirror spill the beans,
Am I now the queen of queens?
Now Snow White's nose is in my tummy,
You must admit I look quite yummy.

But to her horror the mirror replied:

I don't want to shock you, rotten Queen,
But that nose was made of Plasticine.
Snow White's nose is on her face,
She's with some blokes from outer space.

The Mean Queen turned purple. She
smashed the mirror into a thousand
jagged pieces.

Back at the Swinging Spaceship Night
Club, Snow White and the Seven Aliens
had been a huge success. A record producer
had heard them play and signed them on
the spot.

Snow White's dream was coming true.
As Christmas approached, her single 'Snow
White Alien Rap' crept higher and higher
up the charts, eventually even overtaking
Hank Hunk and Boysnog.

Snow White and the Seven Aliens were booked to appear on the Christmas edition of Top of the Pops.

Snow White was terribly nervous. She was sure the Mean Queen would do something to spoil her good fortune. The aliens made her promise to lock her dressing-room door and not let anyone in but them.

But with only half an hour to go before
the programme, someone rattled the door
handle, and a voice called…

Snow White thought the voice sounded a
little strange, but she just had to see if it was
really Hank Hunk from Boysnog come to
see her!

She opened the door a tiny crack.
In burst a tall figure with blonde hair.
It looked like Hank Hunk... But surely
there was something strange about his nose?

Alas! It was the Mean Queen.

When the aliens came to collect Snow White they found her completely frozen with stage fright. No matter how they tried to reassure her, she simply could not move her arms and legs, let alone dance or sing.

In despair, they carried her, like a statue, out of the dressing-room and laid her gently on the stage.

"It's no use," bawled Botty. "We'll have to sing 'hi ho, hi ho...'"

The programme started.

"FAN-TABULOUS Christmas Greetings, pop fans," called the announcer. "We've got a SEN-SATIONAL seasonal line up for you, including the incredible new discovery, Snow White and those Seven EXTREMELY STRANGE Aliens. We've also got Hank Hunk and Boysnog, and later…"

SNOW WHITE
& SEVEN ALIENS

Snow White was still unable to move. To the Seven Aliens, it seemed like a hundred years passed by. Then, at the back of the studio, someone began to push his way through the crowd.

"Let me through," he said. "I'm a qualified heart-throb. I simply must see her."

It was Hank Hunk! This time it really was
him. Snow White's heart began to flutter.

"Oh, Snow White," whispered Hank, "please sing. Sing for me." He bent towards Snow White. A long blonde curl fell across one eye. Gently he kissed her lips.

Snow White leapt to her feet.

"OK BOYS. Let's GROO-VE!!" she shouted.

Snow White and the Seven Aliens leapt into the spotlight and began to play. Across the nation, every family threw down their Christmas crackers and began gyrating to the fantastic sounds on TV.

Everybody, except one person. High in her dark dressing-room, the Mean Queen stared into her shattered mirror and muttered:

Mirror, mirror, smashed to bits,

Today I really feel...the PITS!

But her husband, jiving in front of the TV, called up to her:

That's funny, honey, I feel quite perky,
Come downstairs and have some turkey.
If you're good, you never know,
I might get out the mistletoe.

On New Year's Eve, there were seven special guests at Hank and Snow White's wedding. Their names were Scotty, Spotty, Dotty, Snotty, Potty, Grotty and Botty.

And they all blasted off for a honeymoon in the stars.

"Hi ho, hi ho…"

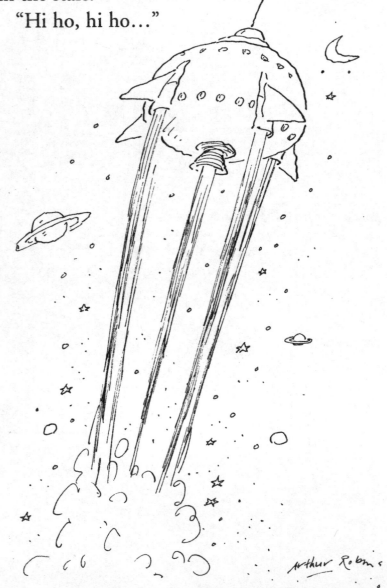